Fabulous Five-Minute Stories

A Night of Nonsense

Written by Jane Arlington

Illustrated by Mike Reid

Reader's Digest Young Families

"Mamaaaaaa! I can't get to sleep!" The loud whine came from the bedroom of the Princess. And it had been coming with great regularity ever since she had been tucked in for the night.

The Queen groaned and stood up from her throne. "This is nonsense!" she declared. "I have opened the window. I have closed the window. I have brought her a goblet of water. What else can be done?"

The King shook his head wearily and passed a hand across his brow. They had been trying to get the Princess to sleep for hours now.

Then he had an idea. "I have it," he said. "I will summon the Royal Musicians."

Moments later the Royal Musicians arrived.

"Play something soft and soothing for the little Princess," implored the King. "Anything to get her to sleep."

The Royal Musicians tiptoed into the Princess's bedroom and began to play. The Princess sat up in surprise when the music began, and then flopped back down onto her velvet pillows. And lovely though the music was, the Princess still tossed and turned.

The Royal Musicians finished their song and tiptoed out of the room. They bowed deeply before the King and Queen, who exchanged hopeful looks.

Just as the King and Queen thought their problem had
been solved, they heard a wail from the Princess's bedroom.

"Papaaaaaa! I can't get to sleep!"

"Oh, no!" said the Queen. "She'll wake the little Prince."

"I shall summon the Jester," said the King.

Soon after that, the Jester bounded into the Princess's bedroom. She sat up in bed and clapped her hands with delight. The Jester did back handsprings. He juggled. He walked on his hands. He swung from his knees.

He grew so weary from performing that he lay down next to the Princess's bed and fell fast asleep.

The Princess, however, did not. Her twisting and turning finally woke the Jester. And he cartwheeled out of the room mumbling, "This is nonsense! And I ought to know!"

Next, the Royal Cook came to the Princess's bedroom. He carried a silver tray with warm milk and chocolate-chip cookies. The Princess ate the cookies and drank the milk. But she did not fall asleep.

"This is nonsense!" said the Royal Cook.

Then the Prime Minister read the Princess a bedtime story in his soft and soothing voice. The Princess listened and yawned. But she did not fall asleep.

"This is nonsense!" said the Prime Minister.

The Ladies in Waiting sang her a lullaby. The Princess sang along. But she did not fall asleep.

"This is nonsense!" trilled the Ladies in Waiting.

Finally, the Royal Magician was summoned. Surely he would have an answer in his bag of tricks. He swept into the Princess's bedroom and sprinkled sleeping dust all over her.

"Did it work?" whispered the King and Queen to the Royal Magician.

He nodded and pointed at the Princess. She lay in her bed with her eyes closed, her breathing heavy and regular.

The King and Queen smiled graciously and presented the Royal Magician with a sack of gold.

"Mamaaaaaa! Papaaaaaa!" cried the Princess.

The King and Queen took back the sack of gold and sent the Royal Magician on his way. Then they walked wearily into their daughter's bedroom.

"My dear, what is the matter?" asked the King. "It is long past your bedtime. You must go to sleep. All of this carrying on is nonsense!"

"I cannot sleep," groaned the little Princess, twisting and turning in her royal bed. "I cannot get comfortable."

Just then, the Royal Nursemaid tapped softly on the door of the Princess's bedroom. "Your Majesties," she said in a quavering voice. "I am so sorry to disturb you, but I have more unsettling news for you. I must tell you that the young Prince has awakened."

The King and Queen groaned.

The little Prince padded sleepily into his sister's bedroom. He stood near the doorway for a moment, watching his sister toss and turn, trying to get comfortable.

Then he gave her a wide smile and walked right over to her bed. He went down on his knees and shoved his little hand under her mattress. He felt around for a moment or two, and he pulled his hand back out.

He knew the cause of all this nonsense! In fact, he was responsible for it.

So he opened his hand to show everyone what he was holding.

It was a pea.

The Princess smiled sweetly and put her head down on her plumped pillows.

"At last, I'm comfy!" sighed the Princess. "Good night, Mama. Good night, Papa," she said sleepily. And one minute later, she was fast asleep.